Augustus Hoppin

Crossing the Atlantic

Augustus Hoppin

Crossing the Atlantic

ISBN/EAN: 9783742864949

Manufactured in Europe, USA, Canada, Australia, Japa

Cover: Foto ©Andreas Hilbeck / pixelio.de

Augustus Hoppin

Crossing the Atlantic

CROSSING THE ATLANTIC

Illustrated by

Augustus Hoppin

Published by
HOUGHTON, Osgood & Co.
BOSTON.

To Capt. Theo. Cook.
of the H.M. ? ? ? M.S.S. Russia.

Dear Capt. Cook:—

"I thank you for allowing me
to place your name on the following page
of my work, & cannot allow the occasion
to go past & silence to hand over unto to
in the honor to receive it, & with also to
ask the privilege of adding unto your com-
mand. To one who has a sense of industry
while in our ? you so showing that I
can add my little artistic ? to reach those
confidence, if I submit under the limitations of
your name."

If "individual sympathy true to all faithful
friends" is the key & faithfulness & that the
friends whom I hear attempted to remind
are all truly imaginary.

Very faithfully yours,
?

LIST OF PASSENGERS BY THE B. & N. A. R. M. S. "ETHIOPIA."

Hon. L. A. Beaconstreet, M. C., and servant,
Mrs. and Miss Beaconstreet and maid, } Boston.

Mr. Brownstone Front and servant,
Mrs. Brownstone Front and maid,
The Misses Front, } children, and nurse, } New York.

Madama Trist, Boulogne.

Sir Mungo Murgatroyd,
Pepper-pot Castle, Hants, England.

Lady Murgatroyd.
Miss Murgatroyd.
Miss Geraldine Murgatroyd.
Master Murgatroyd.
Sir M. Murgatroyd's man-servant.
Lady Murgatroyd's maid.
Rev. Ichabod Barnes, Pohunk, Mass.
Signora Vociferosa, Milan.
Roger Williams Chlam, Rhode Island.
John Smith, Chief of the Senecas.
Oriole Toucan, } Mexico.
Felix Toucan,
Madder Brown, Birmingham.

Mr. and Mrs. John Tobias,
The Misses Tobias,
The Masters Tobias. } Liverpool.

Mr. and Mrs. Wilhelm Spuytenteufel, two children, and nurse, Rotterdam.

P. Malloy, Limerick.

Professor Hare,
Miss Blanche Hare, } Foxboro', Indiana.

Mr. and Mrs. William P. Terrapin, and
Miss Terrapin and Maid, Philadelphia.

Miss Ida Duck and maid, Baltimore.

L. McNamara, Derry.
Miss Jane McNamara, Derry.
Count Perigord, Strasbourg.
Benj. Nevis, Scotland.
A. Pinctre, Raleigh, North Carolina.
Giovanni Macaroni, Naples.
F. Lazzaroni, Naples.
R. Sin, California.
William Nye, Nevada.
Prince Nosemoff, Moscow.
Mr. and Mrs. Asa Smith, }

Van R. Hudson, Albany.

M. Mai-au-Cœur,
Mad. Mai-au-Cœur, } Bordeaux.

Senor Honradez Cigarette, Habana, Cuba.
Mr. Doosle, Bath, Maine.

Harry Wilmer,
Miss Wilmer, } Baltimore.

Hon. Reginald Herbert, and man-servant. } London.

Elder Job. Wilbour and ladies, Salt Lake City.

Mr. and Mrs. S. Sofs, Castile.
Mr. and Mrs. Peter Pops, Rome, N. Y.
Miss Dolly Varden and Maid, England.
R. Van Winkle, Kaatskill, N. Y.

Robert Mavournen,
Miss Kate Mavournen. } Isle of Wight.

A. Skeeter,
Miss Skeeter, } New Orleans.

Mr. and Mrs. Robert Newland, Boston.
Wrynecke Fooks, Berlin.
Walter Gosin, N. Y.

CASTING OFF FROM THE TUG.

"All Aboard!"   "Good-By!"

LIKENESSES OF SOME OF THE PASSENGERS.

1. *Lady Murgatroyd.*
2. *Sir Mungo Murgatroyd.*
3. *Miss Murgatroyd.*
4. *Miss Geraldine Murgatroyd.*
5. *Master Murgatroyd.*
6. *"Toots," the Murgatroyd Dog.*
7. *Sol. Bison.*
8. *Rev. Ichabod Barnes.*

HERE ARE SOME MORE OF THEM.

1. John Smith.
2. One of the Masters Tobias.
3. Hon. Reginald Herbert.
4. Miss Blanche Hare.
5. Benj. Nevis.
6. Harry Wilmer.
7. Elder Job Wilbour.
8. Oriole Toucan.
9. One of the little "Fronts," who keeps us all awake.
10. Miss Dolly Varden.
11. Miss Skeeter.
12. Miss Terrapin.
13. Miss Wilmer.

14. Robert Mavourneen.
15. Miss Jane McNamara.
16. Mrs. Asa Smith.
17. Count Pergord.
18. Signora Vociferosa.
19. Mr. Robert Newland.
20. Mrs. Robert Newland.
21. Mrs. Sope.
22. Signora Vociferosa's puppy, called "Minim."
23. Mr. Terrapin, (who always smokes before retiring.)
24. Giovanni Macaroni.

SAILING DOWN THE MERSEY.

First Dinner. " *All hands*" *at table. Champagne popping, and heads very steady.*

SECOND DAY OUT FROM QUEENSTOWN.

The weather gets "so dirty" that nobody appears at dinner but Mr. Madder Brown of Birmingham, who is making his fifty-third voyage, and who never misses a meal.

A GALE.

(Inside Cabins No. 101 and No. 102.)

The two Misses Murgatroyd prostrate, Lady Murgatroyd considerably discouraged, and Sir Mungo Murgatroyd endeavoring to relieve the distress of his family with a little hot toddy.

UPS AND DOWNS OF LIFE.

(1.) *Sir Mungo, having comforted his family, finds the air of the cabin so " nasty " that he makes all speed for the upper deck.*

(2.) *Meanwhile Brownstone Front, Esq., hurries down to the starboard gangway to Mrs. Brownstone Front and the little Fronts, who are in the spasms of sea-sickness.*

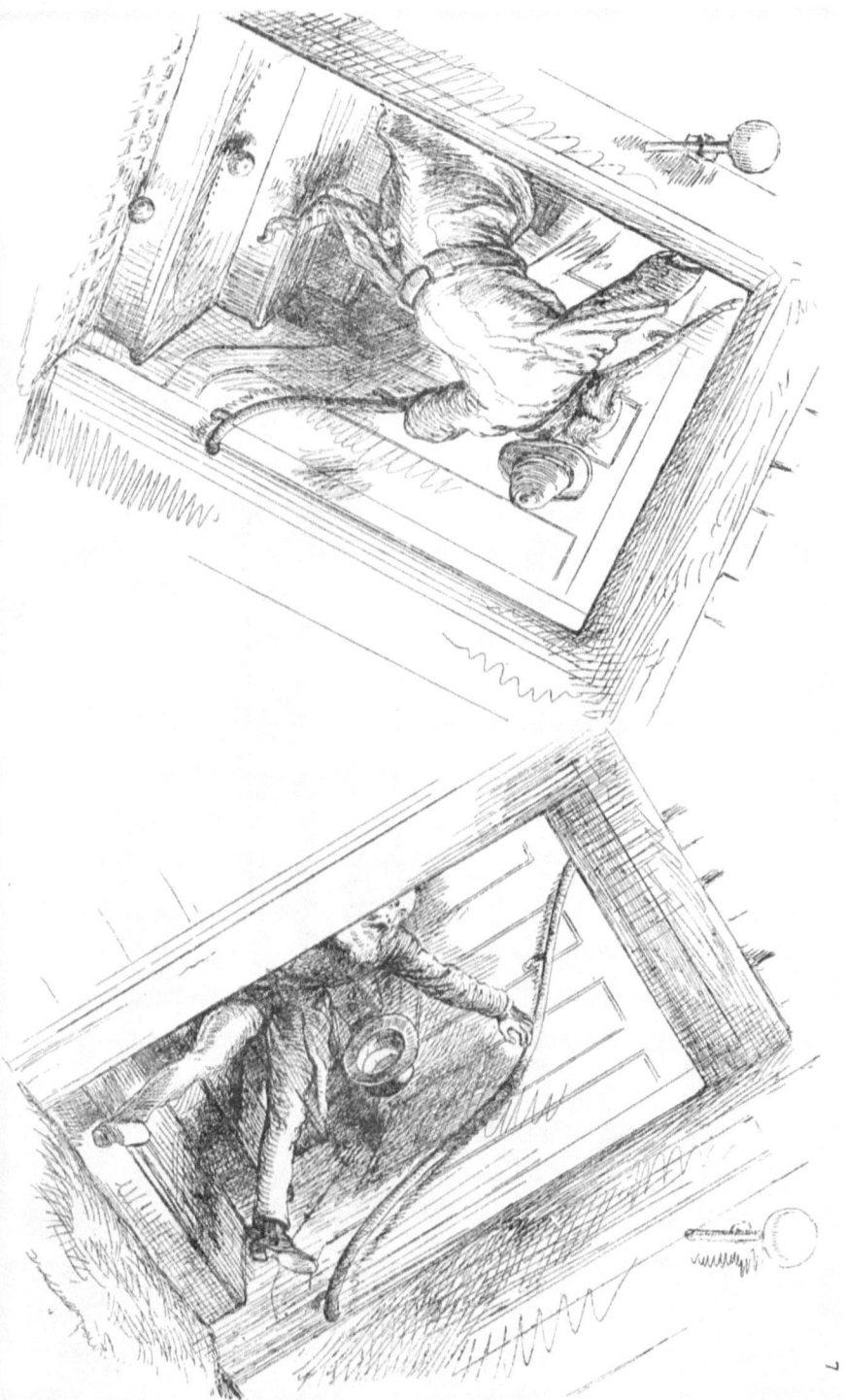

BUSINESS AND PLEASURE.

(1.) *The next morning the sun comes out brilliantly, which induces L. A. Beaconstreet,*
Esq., to make another attempt to get his poor wife on the upper-deck for a
little fresh air. Mrs. Beaconstreet being very sick and very stout, the
operation becomes a serious one.

(2.) *Good-morning, Miss Mavourneen! This lovely creature feels so well that she*
trusts herself to a promenade with the young Englishman from Sheffield.
She finds the "swell" rather agreeable.

ANOTHER FINE MORNING.—HEAVING THE LOG.

The sick ones getting well, and the ship dandling along at fourteen knots.

AFTER LUNCH.

Two of our prime favorites hold their "receptions" on deck.

"BY THE SAD SEA WAVES."

A peep at "Old Ocean" through the port-hole of the cabin.

A COLLISION AT SEA.

The "Goslin" of New York, having lost his "reckoning," overhauls the "Duck" of Baltimore, hoists his signals, and discovers that he is nearer soundings than he expected.

ELEVATION AND DEPRESSION.

(1.) *Rev. Ichabod Barnes, of Pohunk, Massachusetts, feeling particularly frisky, thinks he will expand his chest by climbing the rigging.*

(2.) *Sudden revulsion of Feeling of the Rev. Ichabod after reaching the deck from his dizzy position.*

PLEASANT WEATHER AGAIN.

Playing at " Shuffle—board."

SELLING "POOLS" IN THE "FIDDLE."

Betting on the run of the ship. The Pool on 340 miles bid off at twenty sovereigns. The Rev. Mr. Barnes doesn't dare to go in where they are selling pools, but listens at the door.

(1.) SIGHING FOR LAND.

Signora Vociferosa and dog. "*Oh I wish I vos to my house!*"

(1.) *MORNING.*

The two belles are late at breakfast; and Mr. Van R. Hudson, the Rich young Bachelor from Albany, exhibits his dexterity in making tea from his own "caddy." A noticeable difference between "shore-tea" and "sea-tea."

(2.) *EVENING.*

Game at cards and supper.

MENU.

Broiled Sardines on Toast.

Welsh Rabbit.

Devilled Ham.

Grilled Bones, washed down with Hot Toddy.

SOUNDINGS.

(1.) *A Fog off the Banks.*

(2.) *A dismal group around the smoke-stack before breakfast.*

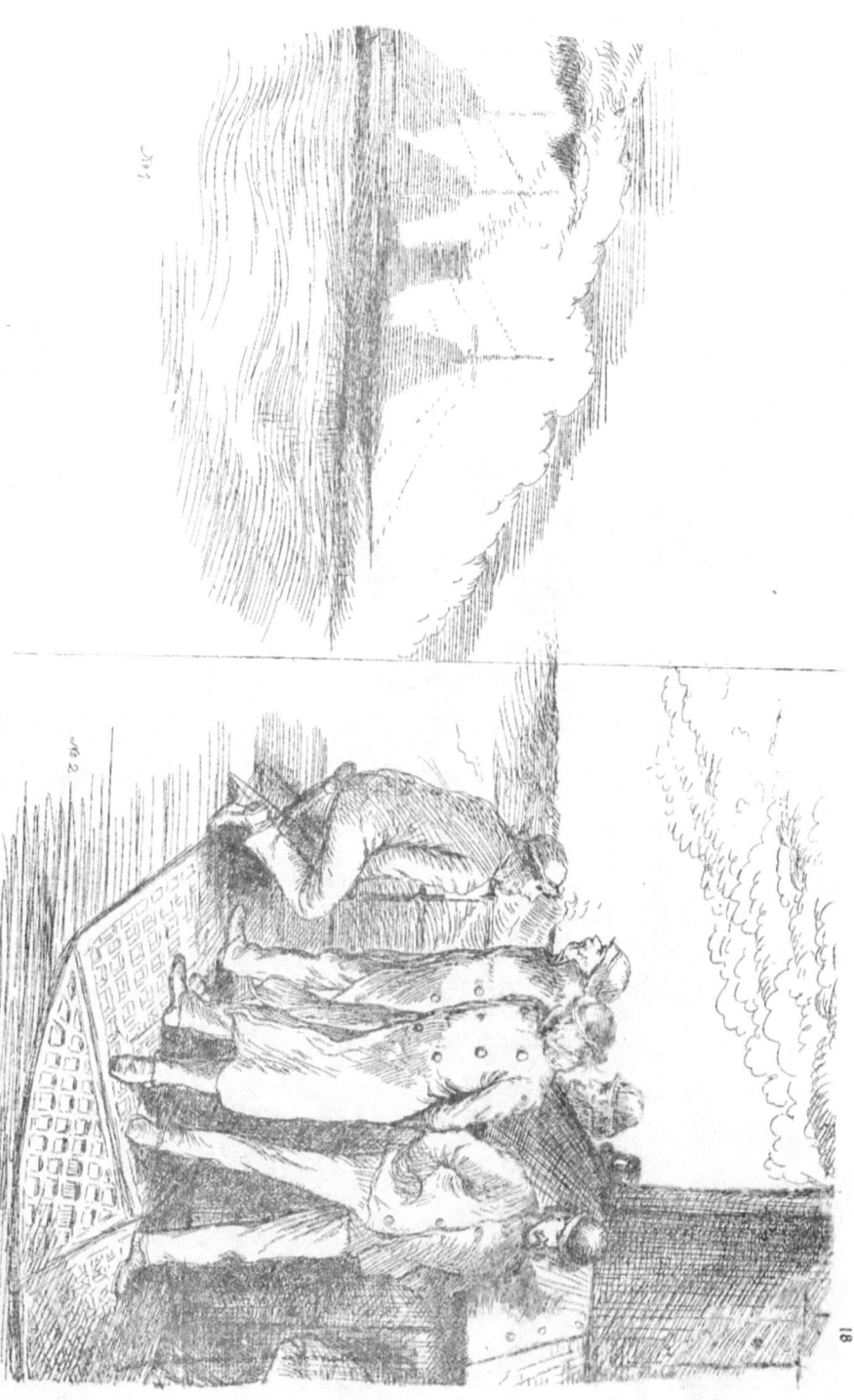

SUNDAY MORNING.

" The Doctor" reads the " English Service."

(1.) *PHOSPHORESCENCE.*

The most favorable time to witness this marine phenomenon is on some starry night in company with a young lady of an inquiring turn of mind.

PILOT BOAT IN SIGHT.

Betting on the number of the boat: "odd or even"; "white hat or black"; "right leg or left first on board."

MAKING PORT.

(1.) *Sudden appearance of stove-pipe hats on the deck,—a sure sign that the voyage is at an end.*

ARRIVED.—SEARCHING FOR LUGGAGE.

The charming Miss Belle Tobias, having lost her twenty-fifth trunk, with no mark upon it, her numerous admirers gallantly offer to hunt it up.

CHART OF THE RUN OF THE SHIP.

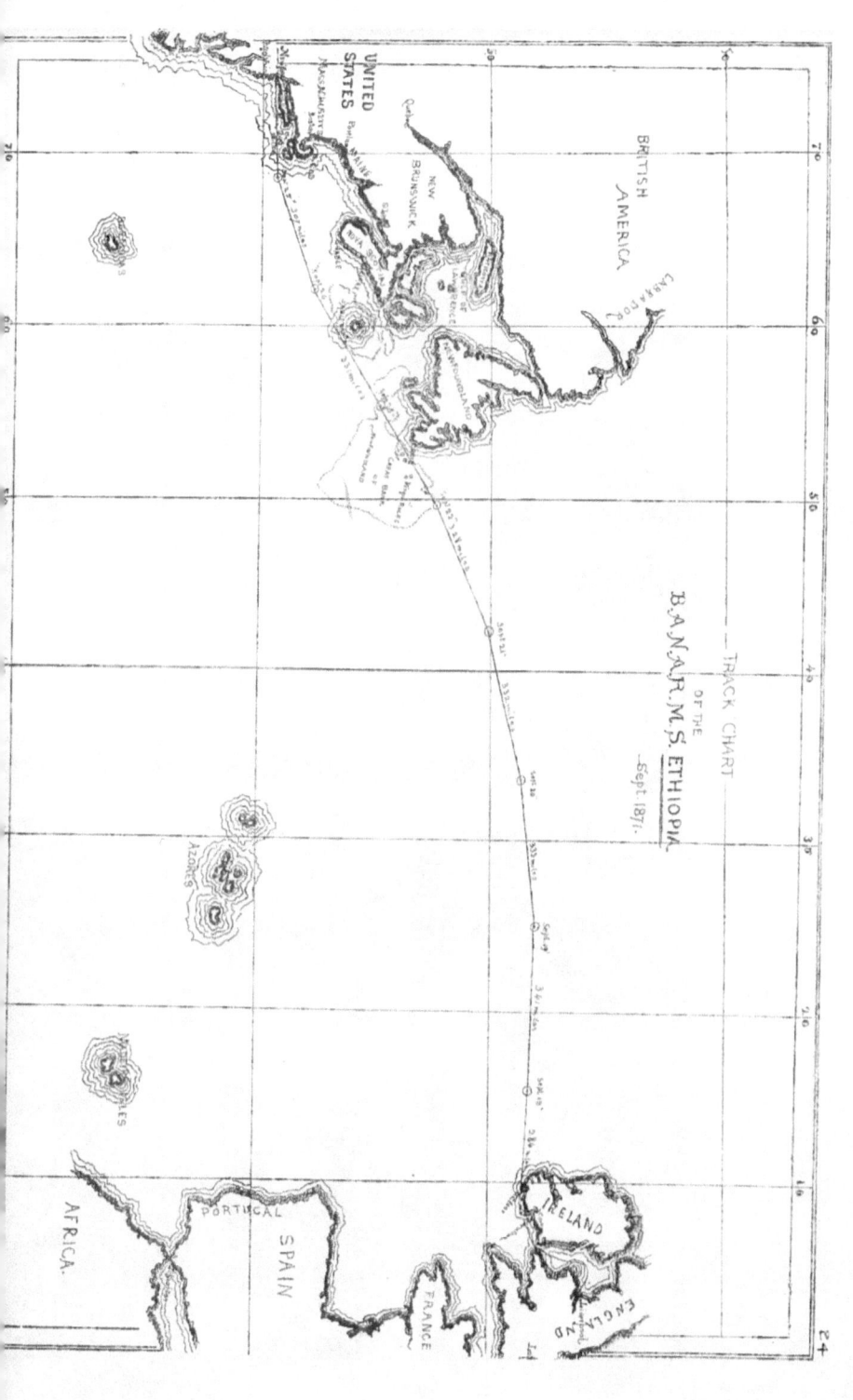

TRACK CHART
OF THE
B.A.N.A.R.M.S. ETHIOPIA.
-Sept 1871-